Sam and Lucy

By Harriet Ziefert   Pictures by Claire Schumacher

HarperCollins*Publishers*

For Fred

Sam and Lucy
Text copyright © 1992 by Harriet Ziefert
Illustrations copyright © 1992 by Claire Schumacher
Printed in Singapore for Harriet Ziefert, Inc. All rights reserved.
1 2 3 4 5 6 7 8 9 10
First edition

Library of Congress Cataloging-in-Publication Data
Ziefert, Harriet.
  Sam and Lucy / by Harriet Ziefert; pictures by Claire Schumacher.
    p.   cm.
  Summary: Two dogs, Sam and Lucy, meet in the park, become mates,
and soon have a litter of puppies.
  ISBN 0-06-026913-8. — ISBN 0-06-026974-X (lib. bdg.)
  [1. Dogs—Fiction.]   I. Schumacher, Claire, ill.   II. Title.
PZ7.Z487Sam   1992   90-46963
[E]—dc20   CIP
                                                               AC

Meet Sam, the best watchdog on Berry Lane.

One morning in early summer Sam decided to take
a vacation and explore the world beyond his yard.

Sam turned the corner and…

kept on going.

Sam was soon out of the neighborhood he knew.

Sam wasn't sure where to go or what to do
so he walked into the park.

Sam tried to make friends with some squirrels.

Then Sam took a nap. When he woke up,
a warm, wet tongue was licking his face.
A small dog with big eyes was being friendly.
Her name tag said, "Lucy."

Sam was hungry. And so was Lucy.
Together they set out in search of food.

Finally, Sam and Lucy came to a delicious picnic.
They feasted on chicken, and peanut butter,
and cookies.

Then they went swimming in the lake.

Sam and Lucy liked each other a lot.
They played tag…

they danced…

they rolled in the dirt…

and they mated.

When night came, they went to sleep under a bench.

The weeks went by.

Sam and Lucy dug for treasure.

On some days Sam went off by himself while Lucy stayed cool under a shade tree. Lucy needed extra rest because she was going to have puppies.

One day Sam came back to find a big surprise.
He saw Lucy with four little puppies!

This one looked just like Lucy.

This one looked just like Sam.

This one looked like Lucy—
but was grey like Sam.

This one looked like Sam—
but was tan like Lucy.

Summer was almost over. Sam wanted to
show off the puppies in his old neighborhood.

So one morning he left the park with Lucy
and the puppies.

Welcome back, Sam!
Welcome, Lucy!
And welcome, puppies!